GW01184947

THE SHOT

A DREAM IN SIX BITS

CONTAINING NO DEPICTIONS WHATEVER OF LUNAR CHEMICAL LABORATORIES

Dedicated to my shooting instructor,
Mr Stewart Wilson
Ye have heard of the patience of Job…..
James 5. 11

DAVID Z CROOKES

All rights reserved. No part of this publication may be reproduced, stored in a retrieval system or transmitted, in any form or by any means, electronic, mechanical, photocopying, recording or otherwise, without the prior permission of the author.

Printed in 2019 by Shanway Press,
15 Crumlin Road, Belfast BT14 6AA

ISBN: 978-1-910044-23-0

© 2019 David Z Crookes

BIT THE FIRST

I bring you no embroidered quips,
I wear a solemn wreath:
I sing of one whose deeds eclipse
The Bathyscape of Beith.
Delilah Robb had ruby lips,
And alabaster teeth;
Like Stiffy Byng, and Stafford Cripps,
She never lived in Leith.
Her father fought on battleships,
And liked the word bequeath;
Her falcon went on foreign trips
With flockth of lithping geethe.

From Headenbirk to Pestabud,
Delilah's name was feared:
She sat for Dellie Roach, but stood
When Chib O'Tellie cheered;
She danced a reel in Birnam Wood
As Tam O'Shanter peered;
She rode to hounds with Robin Hood,
Whom Jack O'Lantern jeered;
She wooed the dreadful Edwin Drood
Until he disappeared —
Enough! My song begins with food,
Which Homer's mind revered.

Delilah wolfed a Welsh meringue,
And washed it down with tea;
At length she read a fierce harangue
By Herbert Hoover Tree.
Her action led a red orang
Utan from Tennessee
To leave his niece in North Penang,
And head for Linden Lea.
Before he caught his plane, he rang
A young performing flea,
And said, 'I hate the whole shebang:
I feel like Sam McGee.'

(Thrasỳmachèan Samothrace
Was fond of Dan Defoe,
Who bought a beetle's carapace
From Edgar Allan Poe.
De Broggly's logarithmic base
Beleaguered high and low:
While Aesop thought it no disgrace
To mention crab or crow,
And Percy French invoked the case
Of Treader versus Toe,
Sorgùmski gave the flea its place
In music, long ago.)

In Rome, the tall orang utan
Was met by Lorna Doone,
Who once complained that Peter Pan
Had bullied Ernest Goon.
She said, 'I flew to Stoke Moran
On Friday afternoon;
Today we need a caravan
To help us reach the moon!
Unless we hatch an oval plan,
We'll win the Wodin Spoon,
For Ludendorff and Suleiman
Have launched a silk balloon.'

The poet William Barnes arrived:
His face was proud and stiff.
'For days,' he said, 'the oxen dived
Without reciting *If*;
For weeks they kept our creeks deprived
Of cruiser, ketch, and skiff;
For months a Jersey heifer jived
Or jigged on Clacton Cliff;
For years I never quite contrived
To glimpse her secret glyph:
Today my pounding heart revived —
I found the Hippogriff.'

'We'll form a group!' the ape replied.
'I came for private ends,
But duty can't be set aside,
In spite of modern trends.
Will Barnes be nitronarkified?
Will Lorna get the bends?
Abandon fear, and don't confide
In quaint loquacious friends!
Orang Utan Guerillas ride
Wherever Fate intends.'
[Terpander pondered. Croydon cried.
The reader comprehends.]

When fair Delilah came aboard
With seven tons of tools,
Her fellow-Fargonauts ignored
The weight-restriction rules.
Their quinquereme serenely soared
Above Saharan pools;
A tightly twisted rubber cord
Enthused the engine-spools.
As Lorna dreamed that gulls were gored
By wild gymnastic bulls,
Delilah dreamed that holes were bored
By gimlet-wielding ghouls.

(Pythagorean wags explain
That once their master wrote
The words *Norwegian, Swede,* and *Dane*
On Lady Luna's coat.
In George the Third's expansive reign,
Lethargic fancy smote
A German baron's quinsied brain,
And made him act the goat.
De Quincey, Quelch, and Quatermain
Were known to quote from Grote!
Our moon has driven men insane:
Beware, in case you dote.)

The guzzler's feast in Gizzard Class
Was Gallic through and through:
Ga-tòe glass-ày, noo-gàh, foo-gàss,
Exquisite *pàt-a-shòe,*
Sicilienne from *Pélleas,*
Daquino's blithe *Coucou,*
With macaroons from Montparnasse,
And prunes from Passepartout.
The steward, Marc-Aurèle Dumas,
Was dressed in Dresden blue;
He kept a pilfered palliasse
In Cabin Number Two.

The pilot, trained by Daniel Dare,
Was Arthur Gordon Pym,
Whom Flerdie Lee and Baudelaire
Confused with Potney Chim.
The autopilot, Rupert Bear,
Was sound in wind and limb;
He lived in Weston-super-Mare,
Beside the River Plym.
The chaplain, Canon Tupperware,
Was dignified, but dim:
He half-believed that Burke and Hare
Were friends of Tiny Tim.

Our heroes flew. Their florid mood
Had banished thoughts of gloom:
They left the lofty dons to brood
On death by sonic boom.
Dumas construed the oiltitude,
Delilah plied her broom,
And Lorna wove a bridal snood
On Lambert Simnel's loom.
Said Pym, 'The view was less than good;
I got my lens to zoom.'
His face was gaunt and sombre-hued:
He whispered, 'Look! A tomb.'

BIT THE SECOND

Its lid obeyed the laws of Hooke,
And bore a vile device:
Above, Anubis weighed a rook
For three balletic mice;
Below, the shaven Pharaoh shook
His hieroglyphic dice.
As Canon Tupperware mistook
The tomb for something nice,
And Lorna Doone prepared to cook
A new spasmodic rice,
Dumas reviewed Nabucco's book
On metamorphic gneiss.

The penteconter's calm descent
Encountered no mischance;
Delilah said, 'I feel content!
We've made a great advance.'
The news was brought to Exe and Brent
By Parker, Field, and Mance;
They rode from Troon to Stoke-on-Trent,
Which then was part of France.
In Cambridge, Cumberland, and Kent,
The press was quick to prance,
And Peer McGinty purred, 'Repent,
Or Annie Traw will dance!'

Dumas demanded ginger beer,
And quaffed a small carafe;
The tariff-laden Tam O'Sphere
Was making Lorna laugh.
When Barnes announced that Paul Revere
Agreed with Franklin Graph,
Delilah said, 'I seem to hear
A Coryphaean calf.'
At once a lunar chanticleer
Applied to join the staff:
Miss Doone remarked that Edward Lear
Employed a toy giraffe.

(The rooster, clad in rustic lace,
Was known as Hielan Jock;
Like Captain Flint, and Colonel Race,
It played the spielenglock.)
As Tupperware began to trace
The roots of French baroque,
Urbane Lornique removed a plaice
From Master Humphrey's Clock!
The Roop recalled that Edgar Cayc-
E goaded Hume and Locke
To use the Parliamentary Mace
In games of Postman's Knock.

Our heroes ran without delay
Toward the Foaming Sea;
If Lorna thought of Hogmanay,
And Pym of perigee,
Delilah thought of Steller's Jay,
And Barnes of kedgeree.
(The healthy mind will often play
With things that disagree:
A smiling vicar dwelt in Bray
Across the road from Smee,
Whose grocer begged Sir Edward Grey
To sit for Klimt and Klee.)

When solar beamlets fell aslant,
The chaplain thought of oil;
He chirped, 'I rant, I pant, I chant!
My guts and gullet boil!
We need a team from West Levant
To ventilate the soil.
I've sent for Uncle Remus, Ant-
Irrhinum, Robert Boyle,
Beluga Whale, Ulysses Grant,
Aquinas, D'Arty Coyle,
Von Hügel, Paley, Whistler, Kant,
And Arthur Conan Doyle.'

Delilah Robb was unimpressed
With Tupperware's tirade;
She said, 'You ought to take a rest;
Your nerves are badly frayed.
Although you've done your level best,
Your Proper Nouns Parade,
For all its length, has not addressed
The terms of lunar trade.
I yearn to buy hotels on Leicest-
Er Square. Be nòt afraid!
The Archimedes Palimpsest
Implies a masquerade.'

The poet muttered, 'What we need
Is first the Morning Post,
And then a Gàrantùlic feed
Of bacon, eggs, and toast.
My words are very wise indeed,
And that is not a boast!
I've planted woad and tumbleweed;
I've plucked a crowd or host
Of daffodils in Runnymede:
I've grilled the Monday roast.
I've smuggled mead for Adam Bede,
And salt for Pepper's Ghost.'

Our friends, inflamed by appetite,
Attacked their meal with zeal.
Delilah claimed that Wilbur Wright
Had flown from Lille to Kiel,
While Orville toured the Isle of Wight
In search of jellied veal.
Said Pym, 'Their planes were put to flight
By Chief Inspector Teal,
But Martin Rattler won the right
To meet Sir Ferris Wheel
When Simon Templar picked a fight
With Norman Vincent Peale.'

'It goes to prove,' the steward sighed,
'That mulish common sense
Will formulate formaldehyde
Without uncouth expense.
Sir Euroclydon Ophicleide
Provides a clear defence
For Patrick Spence, who petrified
The future perfect tense.
Will Tom perform *The Bartered Bride*
In front of Polly's fence?
Has Piglet Pleaser prophesied
A peg to Peter's Pence?'

'Forget your thrifty coins of brass!'
The rural canon roared.
'You've missed the point, and sold the pass,
By falling overboard.
Can Tallis tell the Pontal Ass
That Rip van Winkle snored?
Should Cinderella, shod with glass,
Regale the Golden Horde?
Will Fosco, Tosca, Hood, and Vas-
Co hide the minted hoard
Of Mother Goose and Noble Gas
In Handel's harpsichord?'

'You lack the Flint of Sincostan!'
Corelli bellowed back.
'Sylvànus Penn, the Inkermann,
Promoted Knife the Mac,
And Corvid Matthew gave Milan
A young Tibetan yak.
I've neither seen a copper flan,
Nor heard a nickel quack;
I'm not a torpid Also Ran:
I've crawled on bladderwrack!
I've trawled the Trent with Grafter Vann,
And brawled with Brendan Brack—'

BIT THE THIRD

'Enough! We're tired of Gothic type!'
Delilah yelled in rage.
'Your trains of thought are full of tripe!
You sound like Percy Flage!
Will Dance Micawber pay the pip-
Er's hyperbolic wage?
Did Cuff and Candy stuff a snipe
With onion, pork, and sage?
Is Plato Pluto? Either wipe
The slate, or turn the page.
Your grapes of wrath are more than ripe,
So kindly leave the stage.

'A humming-bird like Hemingway
Will fix your Pisan tilt
When Faraday and Caraway
Can dine with Dinah Quilt.
I wonder now if lunar clay
Contains Nilotic silt.'
The chaplain squawked in sheer dismay,
'I feel my fingers wilt!
As Bax alleged on Boxing Day,
The Taj Morale was built
By Dan McGrew and Thomas Gray
To house the works of Milt—'

'On guard!' said Pym. 'The *Golden Hind*
Was never known to flee;
Her thick manila sails were lined
With twill by Tweedledee.
Allergic Doggy-Knees defined
The numbers *i* and *e*
As tricks that Oiler's wicked mind
Had played on forty-three.
The humble *pi* was left behind
By Maupassant de Guy,
Whose gallimaufry undermined
The gaudy fraud in *She*.

'A store of true Gaufrìdic lore
Was mulled or multiplied
By Murgatroyd of Ruddigore,
Whom Ludd annoyed in Ryde.
The skulking culprit primly swore
That Celts would rule the Clyde,
And vowed that ravens nevermore
Would roost in Kelvinside.
A kilted boar from Bangalore
Emerged at Lammastide,
And bit the butler's battledore
While Jekyll joked with Hyde.'

'But William Tell,' said Tupperware,
'Was academic dean
When Para Handy held the chair
Of Greek at Aberdeen.
His Aunt Amarna bought a mare
From Alfie Lamartine,
And sold the foal in Finisterre
To monumental Migne.
Before she clobbered Angel Clare,
Amarna helped Racine
To make a film that showed her flair —
The Nuns of Skibbereen.

'She led a noisy bugle-band
From Crumplehorn to Crewe;
She redesigned the Krugerrand,
And poisoned Mr Pugh.
(Her second film, *The Gelded Land*,
Was shot in limbic Looe;
The rôle of Mr Chips meand-
Ered back to Philip Dru.)
Amarna's films were often banned —
Beguiled in Bakerloo,
The Scallywags in Samarkand,
And *Guilt* in Sutton Hoo.

'Amarna's colleague, Kellogg Pact,
Became Crimean Khan
When Simon Bocanegra backed
The Rhinns of South Piranh;
A Brontë came to Pontefract
With poor Ca-cà-li-bàn,
And tore Papyrus Hepteract
From Gurkha's new divan.
Sir Flinders Dish composed a tract
On Lady Bindle's fan,
In which he pointed out the fact
That Metz was not Sedan.

Von Epp, the Cuban epicure,
Encouraged Gossip Joan
To call the Beast of Bodmin Moor
An Appaloosa roan!
(The unobtrusive ligature
Of Tyne and Rhine and Rhône
Identified her signature
As Anglosaxophone.)
Both Coop de Grass and Soop de Joor
Abjured the Thracian throne,
But Turandot could not endure
Their domineering tone.

'The case developed. William Tell
Deboojumized a Snark;
Godiva's dental diving-bell
Alarmed the Gentle Lark.
MacBogateer de Bagatelle
Forbade his dog to bark;
A Polish choir equated Pell
With Jeremiah Clarke.
Sir Flinders floundered. Alf Nobel
Had sharply hit the mark!
The selling price of marble fell
To farthings. Days were stark.

'When Leithen, Lugg, and Sugg perceived
The scale of Scudder's deed,
They left their field of corn unsheaved,
And bombed St Mary Mead.
A rhombic rambler soon retrieved
The trove of Harris Tweed,
Whose craven creed was not believed
By Ravenscroft and Ede.
Sir Nigel Gresley, unaggrieved
By Mallard's turn of speed,
Enjoyed *Success de Steam*, which peeved
Amarna's mournful steed.

'Baguettes were set in wicker packs
Beside the Bridge of Tay;
Cheroots were put in ricks or stacks
Of dry bedraggled hay.
As Locatelli's liquor-tax
Dissolved in disarray,
The Steepadilly Picklejacks
Invaded Eriskay.
A shell exploded. Sticklebacks
Inveighed against the sleigh,
But sycophantic Sycorax
Applauded Florence Kraye.

'The muse of Jenner, Joule, and Verne
Was Pell's impulsive niece;
She clinched a deal with Lady Fern,
And pinched the Golden Fleece.
Did Mrs Grundy's groom discern
The gramophones of Greece?
Should Bernadotte have gone to Bern,
And told the Swiss police?
Will Cavaletti never learn
To live in blissful peace?
It's hard to tell. I often yearn
For pants without a crease.'

BIT THE FOURTH

Our canon stopped. A lunar gale
Enblew. The rooster crowed.
Aeòlus bade his cronies wail
Their dark Pindaric ode.
As Nayland Smith annulled the stale
Napoleonic Code,
A storm of stalactital hail
Engulfed the Guelphic Road.
Delilah froze. Her cheeks were pale;
She dòh-ray-mè-fah-sòhed,
'Fashòda tactics never fail:
Remember Mr Toad.

'Forgotten blue pagodas meet
My giddy human gaze:
I see a fire of lunar peat,
I hear Zohàric lays,
I smell Siroccan sugar-beet,
I taste Moroccan maize.
Exhort your tired unhappy feet
To hope for better days:
You're bound to get a bit of heat
By sitting near the blaze;
We mustn't bush around the beat,
Like pesky Pàscal Blaise.

'When Rowland Hill began to tame
The Holy Roman See,
His droll quadrille became a game
Of golf with Gusty Bea.
Astilbe told her clique to blame
The Sheikh of Arabee!
Ketèlbey, Tull, and Tyler came
From frenzied Innisfree
To seek the busy dame whose name
Was Lizzie Barrett Leigh.
(A single-barrelled Henry Jame
Deciphered Ventris B.)

'If Slope and Slocum fill the Slade
With men like Jervis Fen,
Effendi's dervish-led brigade
Will count from one to ten.
Sir Vagus Nerve may well evade
Minerva's fountain pen!'
Our friends approached a rich arcade,
Designed by Cactus Wren,
To find that Dr Dee had made
Its vault the vulture's den
In which he brewed or bred or brayed
Quaternal aitch with en.

The wizard spoke. 'I got my jade
From Ebenezer Prout,
Whose brother Pontifex displayed
The classic signs of gout.
Their sister, Mrs G Lestrade,
Released a jussive lout
When Joseph Priestley's lemonade
Was laced with lactic stout.
Her Gallowegian gallopade
Inspired the Canning Spout;
In later life, she taught the Maid
Of Perth to catch a trout.

'(Did Merthyr Tydfil send a swarm
Of bees to Bantry Bay?
Will furtive Archie Plute inform
The gruesome Agnes Grey?)
Sir Panty Grool and Rant O'Corm
Purloined a pewter tray;
Belinda Pocket found a dorm-
Ant earl in Erskine May!
In nimble Vietnam, a gorm-
Less horse began to neigh;
The Troglodytes betrayed enorm-
Ous leeks in Lake Mêlée.

'On yellow sloops and blue corvettes
The dour Venetian Dog
Would lay his bets, and pay his debts
With double tots of grog.
Milady's loud melodic threats
Enthralled a frugal frog,
Who threw rabbinic banjo-frets
At Captain Smollett's log.
She told cadets in Codesy-Betts
That Haig would road the hog
If Rider Haggard's baronetc-
Y fell to Filey Fogg.

'But Banker Dogg and Ballantyne
Forgot Milady's jest!
The Litmus Test of Liechtenstein
Was failed by Fielder Chest;
His wife relieved their washing-line
Of jerkin, shirt, and vest,
So Perkin's ginger porcupine
Was very badly dressed.
A crested robin crossed the Rhine,
And built her gnostic nest
In bashful Ashton-under-Lyne,
Where dates and figs are pressed.

'Sir Edward Goschen came to spar
With Señorita Gish;
Ignatius Grubb was met by Clar-
Ice Cliff in Serbic Nish;
Convulsive Mr Valdemar
Evinced the vulgar wish
That Marlin Spike of Mullingar
Would feed the cuttlefish.
(His injudicious ginger-jar
Had come with Flinders Dish!)
Tecùmseh Lutwidge lent his car
To clumsy Wendell Bysshe.

'Affairs were tangled. Tongan fears
Increased from week to week.
Lalique departed. Guilty peers
Conversed in stilted Greek.
Boleyn belayed her pin. Emìrs
Immured the Bibbly Theek.
Tagòre's oblique Moluccan gears
Were locked in meek Belleek;
Angoran goats created piers
By night in Martinique,
And Monopods with garden shears
Invented – yes! – the breek.

'"Rebuke Rebecca!" squealed a Czech.
"Her squalid book condemns
Contorted buckles, North Quebec,
The stork, and scalloped hems."
A scandal followed. Alan Breck
Had sworn to swim the Thames;
He looked in ev'ry raucous wreck
For gold-encrusted gems,
And always checked beneath the deck
For pipes with amber stems.
The thing that made him risk his neck —
A telegram from Ems —

'Was found in fiendish Tenerife
By William Joynson-Hicks,
Whom Dr Locke appointed chief
Of staff in 'twenty-six.
Sagacious Gosling guessed that Boeph-
E baffled Pharaoh Hyks;
Osiris Mimble pelted Crieff
With pentahedral bricks.
(Her curried beef defied belief!
The troopers played their tricks,
But all in vain.) She caught a thief,
And drained the River Styx.'

BIT THE FIFTH

Delilah slept. Ran-Gùta closed
His narcoleptic eyes.
The rooster slumbered. William dozed.
The pilot dreamed of pies.
The weeping steward juxtaposed
A flux of noes and ayes;
He sobbed, 'The wizard must have hosed
My head with liquid lies.'
An awkward Lorna diagnosed
Her friends with frank surprise,
And asked, 'Has Dee morphètamòsed
Our fatal new disguise?

'Annihilation waits for Jill
If Jack deplores the well;
A diet based on chlorophyll
Is bad for Little Nell.
Will gelid books like *Flossie Mill*
Enable bees to spell?
Does Archimedes need a drill?
Did Carmen stab Ravel?
A village oaf can link Seville
With Savile Row. Rebel!
Sophisticated Clabber Hill
Is merely Clever Hell.'

'Lornique,' the Roop declared, 'your gust
Of speech was quite robust!
Both Cheke and Pusey feel disgust
For gastrophilic lust,
And Peekaboo's eternal blust-
Er seldom earns a crust.
The frequent use of words like just
Betokens mental rust:
If bleak elusive trees are trussed
By rhyme and metre, trust
In truth receives a sabre-thrust,
And deacons bite the dust.'

'Combustive Bear,' said Dr Dee,
'Your fusty monochrome
Befits a realm where fiddlers three
Demote the metronome.
If Sadducee and chimpanzee
Seduce your temple-dome,
The mighty Muffin Man is free
To ream and rhyme and roam!
Does Titus Puffin bow the knee,
Or vow to stay at home?
Beware the crone whose wan decree
Divorces *team* and *tome*.

'(At night, in bed, we all engage
With Snarks of many kinds;
Our Bàphomètic Lodgers wage
Their war on wary minds.
Sir Bofe MacSodge controls the cage;
Eccentric Hilbert grinds
A torrid barrel-organ. Maj-
Or Biff O'Natchie finds
Rebuff in chordal Cardiff. Traj-
An tramples Troy! He winds
A semi-hunter. Narrow gauge
Is back. Diana binds

'A stook in Stephen Foster's field,
Or weds a wooden spouse,
Whose wading boots are soled and heeled
By vernal Colonel House.)
When Faust MacPhistoe first revealed
The orbal strain of Strauss,
Laforgue annealed a corgi-shield,
And healed the Regal Mouse.
Odile's illegal dollar sealed
The fate of Hazel Grouse;
In Gothenburg, the bells were pealed
By Gutenberg and Gauss.

'Let Garrideb corroborate
The rowdy treble chime!
You get my point. Our painted gate
Can make Lepanto mime,
And Cowdenbeath may denigrate
Belgrade. Has Father Time
Debowdlerized a bardic date?
Rejoice in Regis Lyme!
Forsake the Socratean crate
Of feeble fables. Climb
A hillock. (Dull idyllic pat-
Riotic thought is crime.)

'Import an orchid. Fly to Crete
With choral kittiwakes.
Salute a scarlet parakeet.
Explore Minorcan lakes.
Obliterate the sheep who bleat
On parchment. Grin like snakes,
Or march with inward larches. Greet
Elected frozen hakes.
Impignorate repugnance! Eat
Amỳgdalàceous Cakes.
Emprison Burke. Embark a fleet
Of Izzenbirks. The brakes

'Are off! Tobogganeering sleep
May crave an eerie death;
Pandora's ògham-stave will steep
Your young in bearish breath.
An ogre braves the brutal deep
Where newts engender BETH:
His gamma-rays of doom can leap
From Digby's dogma. (TETH
Is nine, as Tethys knew! I weep
To think that Coptic HETH
Was cooped in jail.) Cajole the keep
Of Horus, Thoth, and Seth.

'How others land…..' KerBANG! The shot
Disrupted Jaundie's fun:
A reader, tired of tommy-rot,
Had fired her tommy-gun.
The nettled carbineer was not
A Carmelitish nun;
She said, 'An *i* without a dot
Is Turkish. Minus one,
The square of *i*, completes the plot.'
(Who punished Mr Pun?
A Stornawegian polyglot,
Whose name was Sally Lunn.)

'We ought to leave,' said Lorna Doone,
        'Before the lads allude
To Johnny's, well, *sepulchral swoon*,
        And Sally's pulchritude.
        (I've allocated Al Ö'Coon
        To look for Dorffenlud;
The Dufflepuds will soon maroon
        Morose moronic Frude.)
We'll never find a Moon Saloon!
        Our present neighbourhood
Evokes a crudely drawn cartoon
        Of Budapest, or Bude.

'We've mauled the man who went to mow,
        We've bawled at Lochinvar;
We've burgled barn and bungalow,
        We've gargled purple tar.
A year ago, in Plymouth Hoe,
        We stole the Hamilcar,
And sailed along the silken Po
        To pelvic Zanzibar.
The twytte thatte wrytte *below, below*
        Can see how smart we are:
Unquell the knell! We need to go —
        It's time to cross the bar.'

BIT THE SIXTH

Ignition! Pym's Homeric boat
Began its homeward race.
Reclusive Rupert cleared his throat,
And growled, 'I beg your grace!
The telescopes are taking note;
We'll deck the quarter-pace.
Our adjectival anecdote
Should rival *Chevy Chase*.'
[Attila dropped a silver groat
On Tully's pòjum-dace;
Poppaea watched a vessel float
In popliteal space.]

Delilah made a chequered mat
From newly heckled flax,
But William dipped the vittle-vat
In votive candle wax.
As Lorna lit her ziggurat
Behind the lintel-racks,
She trilled, 'A Theban diplomat
Maligned our mintoshacks!
If Trumper's bat and Trilby's hat
Bemuse the jumberlacks,
Sir Warden Glebe will help to plait
Their glib and gleeful tracks.'

'You ought,' responded Pym, 'to say
Your piece in Vedic Norse;
Our stowaway from Stornaway
Believes in lethal force!
Her blunderbuss, which Marshal Ney
And Nye O'Marsh endorse,
Will undercut the Quai d'Orsay
By firing twigs of gorse.
Sir Machrihanish Ronaldsway
Has never shown remorse
For using vintage Beaujolais
To dope the Trojan Horse.

'Did Mary Rudge or Wallis Budge
Admire the Queen of Tyre?
Should Clytemnestra blend her fudge
With Heraclitan fire?
Will pterodactyls dare to judge
A sparrowhawk's attire?
The narrow-minded Mr Sludge
Can leer at Nero's lyre:
When Simple Simon tries to trudge
Across the Grimpen Mire,
O'Grady holds a bitter grudge,
And Byron builds a byre.

'Torquato Tasso won the toss:
He taught Matisse to smoke.
Sargasso borrowed Carabosse,
And Barbarossa woke.
A Saragossan albatross
Was crass enough to croak
That Gloucester Cheese and Worcester Sauce
Would nourish country folk.
The Dorset painter, Henry Gosse,
Remained in Gospel Oak!
Sarastro lost a corset. Nos-
Tradamus pestered Polk…..'

'Or Pocahontas!' howled the ape.
'(Her dripping cloak was dried
By Maccabeus Masking-Tape,
Whose bailiff bowled a wide.)
Tibullus built a fire-escape,
And caught the Cornish tide
Before Debrett procured a drape
For Snap the Dragon's bride.
A comic sniper came to Snape,
Where torus knots are tied;
He shot a numismatic shape,
And died of coincide.'

'His barcarolle,' said Marc-Aurèle,
'Was rudely disenrolled
When Brunelleschi brought Brunel
To Joseph Nettlefold.
(Clarissa, Maud, and Claribel
Had made the clouds unfold!)
De Nesselrode and Beau Brummel
Embraced the winter cold;
Their non-Cartesian toll-cartel
Maintained a stranglehold
On Scarabaean scallopshell
And Caribbean gold.'

'Correct!' said Pym. 'Charybdis felt
That bulky Walter Crane
Would Balkanize Vanilla's Belt,
And beat the Lesser Wain.
Decrepit Woonie Spiller dealt
A crow to Blazy Jane;
St Elbow sent his fire to melt
The Burma-frost in Spain.
Pyloric Nestor's panther-pelt
Was torn by Thomas Paine,
Yet Yorick, Blake, and Euclid knelt
With Drake on Drury Lane.'

Our friends could feel the turpentine
Of atmospheric cloud;
Machete numbers eight and nine
Beshrewed the mizzen-shroud.
The flügel-horn produced a whine:
The ailing hinges ploughed
Their weary way to Townachine —
Unbloodied, yes, but bowed.
When Spanker Boom and Frankenstein
Exclaimed, '*E-am-us-gaud!*',
Miss Lunn replied, 'Your plodding line
Will never draw a crowd.'

The undercarriage juddered. Pym
Was tense. He steered his craft
With care. A wanton zephyr's whim
Created grief abaft.
Eliza Scudder's *Vesper Hymn*
Was warbled. No one laughed.
Lieutenant Lunn, whose face was grim,
Begripped her dagger-haft,
And read a yarn by Nicky Klimm.
(Dumas was keen to graft
A hybrid tea from Crater's Rim
For William Howard Taft.)

Delilah's team was home at last!
As Pym debriefed the press,
His autopilot fled aghast
From Goody Blake's caress.
The rooster ate a light repast
Of crab with clove and cress;
Niquòler strove to flabbergast
The Jabberwock with chess.
Sir Cantilever Counterblast
Observed, *'N'oblige oblesse!'*
Quoth Barnes, 'Avaunt, thou podrogast!
Thy hawkish name is Jess.'

A quadruped from Petrograd
Betrod Alaskan lawns;
Alonso found a lake where Vlad
Tsepèsh had fed the swans.
Neruda's afternoon charade
Included lunar fauns.
Bermuda glowed. The moon was glad.
Miss Doone redeemed her pawns.
Delilah made a flooring brad
From mango-flavoured bronze.
Our sturdy chaplain works in Chad,
But stop! The reader yawns.